THE BOGEYMAN:

True Confessions of a Golf Addict

Ilee Coleman

Acknowledgements

I would like to say thanks to everyone who has ever supported me in one way or another; either through the purchase of this book or the experience within our friendships. I would like to open my heart to GOD and allow him to look deep into my soul and know how much I value our personal relationship. Special thank you to the Coleman-Ward-Denton-Hayes-Gaymon-Hicks-Warren-Beck-Robinson-Davis-Williams-Fairley families. We may be spread out but we are always spiritually connected.

To my parents James and Linda there is nothing more powerful than I love you. Thanks to my brother for introducing me to my nephew Denim a.k.a. Jay 2

There are three things that I love more than anything in this world and they are Saijah, Nadja and Ilee jr.

To my wife of countless years, I knew from the start that we were meant to be. Without your superhuman strength to hold me up whenever I fell, I would not have made this accomplishment. You are my eternal gift of hope and happiness. I love you more than you could ever know.

*R.I.P: James and Nettie Ward my heart aches for you as I miss you every day. Ruth Gaymon I love you and miss us eating our chicken wings together.

Chapter 1

The Offering

"You can't be serious…GOLF??? Get the hell outta here with that bullshit! Out of the blue you want to be Tiger Woods? How do you go from jockin' Michael Jordan to Tiger Woods in a day? Especially after you learned that his wife picked up a 9-iron and beat his ass from 100 yards in! Well, not me my brother. NOT ME!!!"

Holding onto the other end of the phone was one of my best friends, Steve, who is always venturing out to do new things and meet new people. I sarcastically laughed at this latest endeavor where he had committed himself and three others to participate in a charity golf event at one of the prestigious west Florida golf courses. His commitment to a cause usually means that a recruitment of his brethren is soon to follow. You have to give a huge *kudos* to Steve for wanting to give back; but who wants to spend the day with a bunch of stuffy, stuck-up folks?

"C'mon man! It'll be fun! We'll hang out for the day, have dinner and drinks, rub elbows with some potential door-openers, and at the end of the day it's all for a good cause!"

Steve began to go into sales mode. A natural salesman at heart, he proceeded to spew out all the benefits of attending the charity golf event.

I replied, "I don't know how to play golf and it looks really boring. I don't see how swinging a steel stick through grass and hitting a little white ball towards an itty-bitty hole in the ground is…FUN. Plus, I don't want to be out in that sweltering Florida heat. You know we are supposed to be flammable."

Through the receiver I heard Steve chuckle, and then, following a brief silence, he uttered the words which would ultimately seal the deal, "Well, you know Donnie and Marcus are going and…."

I sat up and asked, "Donnie and Marcus are going?"

"Yeah!" said Steve, "And you know how Donnie is. He's already started running his mouth and we've still got another three weeks until the event!"

Donnie, Steve and I have been friends for years and just recently we added Marcus to the "Band of Brothers". Donnie truly is the undisputed poster boy for sarcasm. He is very opinionated, loud, funny at times and has a monstrous head like the Fred Flintstone cartoon character – hence the name of his alter ego – "Fred-Head". Marcus, the youngest of the group and the recipient of many of Donnie's off-the-wall wise cracks, is a fitness fanatic. He stays in youthful shape and is a dark-skinned man with noticeably white teeth. Toss into the mix that he's always as hyper as a kid who overdosed on sugar candy and you can understand why I nicknamed him, "Black Lalane" (a play on the name of the late fitness guru, Jack Lalane).

Steve, who I pegged with the name, "Gazoo" (the magical little friend of Fred Flintstone with the enormous helmet and miniature body), knew that any afternoon outing that included the 'Four Musketeers', dinner and a brew would be appealing to me because whenever we are all together a simple gathering can easily become a lifelong memorable adventure!

"OK! I'll go, but since you and Donnie have played before you got to cut us some slack as I don't want to look like a fool out there."

"Don't worry!" said Steve, "We're playing in a Scramble format, so it's team play."

"Team play sounds more like it. I'll talk with you later." I hung up the phone.

Stunned at what I had just committed to I turned on the television and tried to watch a little bit of a professional golf tournament but found it excruciatingly boring to say the least. I absolutely had no interest in it. I grew up in a large New York City housing tenement where contact sports were a way of life and the physical and mental challenges continued far away from the courts or fields. I was used to basketball, football, and boxing, where you man up to your opponents, use stifling defense to shut them down, whisper *un-sweet* nothings into their ears and release a barrage of offensive weaponry to gain an edge. Then as the time clock buzzes, you turn to your opponent, thanking him/her for participating and raise your hands signaling to everyone that you are the victor. What I was watching on TV wasn't *ANY* of that. It was too calm, too orderly and quietly poker-faced.

Fans cheered as if they were in a library and were acknowledged with a tilting of a hat or a gentle finger wave by the participating so-called athletes.

What kind of sport was this and why would anyone with any competitive spirit or real athletic prowess want to watch or play it? This is not even a *REAL* sport. Its design is clearly intended for the athletically challenged *"yuppies"* who wipe their sweat with green eagled paper. It's for those Perrier water drinkers who prefer unspotted glasses to frosty mugs. It's for the little big men who secretly suffer from Napoleon complexes. You've seen the humongous cars on the road where the person driving seems to be making love to the steering wheel and the driver's seat is completely visible through the window. This is not for me!

DEFINITELY!....NOT FOR ME!

Later that evening, while sitting on the couch with my wife and pretending to channel surf, I finally settled on the NBA games (which had been my intent all along). See, changing the channel directly to sports without being considerate of what she wanted to watch would trigger a conversation that I didn't want to participate in. So, while I'm strangling the "up" button on the cable remote, I make a quick stop at *The Home Shopping Network,* and then a brief pause to see what drama is occurring on *Basketball*

Wives. This route always makes the final destination much more palatable for her and equally satisfying for me.

During the half-time commercial break I leaned over and playfully said to her, "Do I look like someone who would play golf?"

She cut her eyes left, squinted, shrugged her shoulders and a little crease appeared on her forehead as she uttered, "I don't know. What does a person who plays golf look like?"

Immediately an awkward pause entered the room and sat down in between us, and I casually leaned left to give it some space.

She continued, "OH LORD! What are you and the other three dudes from the Discovery Channel up to?"

"Ah, you got jokes!" I said, "Steve asked me to play golf in a charity event with him and I believe the whole crew is going to be involved. I don't really want to go."

She quickly replied, "But it's for charity and you would be experiencing something new with your friends. You should be thankful that someone thinks enough of you to invite you. Broaden your horizons. You never know…You may even like it!"

I immediately gave her the "I just smelled rotten eggs in a jar" face. Did she just say I may like it? Is she crazy? I dare not say out loud what I was thinking because whenever my wife hits me with, "Be thankful for…", any response other than "You're so right" is followed by, "You're being selfish" or, "You are so blind to the blessings you receive". Even though she might be a little bit on the correct side, that was *NOT* what I was looking for. I needed her to jump in my lap on this matter and respond favorably with, "What?? Golf?? Is he serious??"

The next day I got a call from Fred Head and he went in right from 'Hello'.

"You know they hold charity events like this just to make everyone else feel better when they give *me* the trophy, dawg! Everybody else is just an extra for the champion's parade. Your lovely wife probably told you to be thankful, didn't she? What you NEED to be thankful for is the fact that you're on the team with the winner!"

Just like Fred to stir the pot. His sarcastic humor sets the stage for all events to follow. With Fred's backdrop of narration and his ability to create anticipation, I felt myself begin to slip down the rabbit hole to Wonderland; and he was definitely the Mad Hatter! As he continued to express his anticipated delight of an afternoon of fun with the guys, he also slid in a sidebar remark to spark my competitive juices, "Just make sure you bring a bunch of balls for yourself because you're gonna need 'em!"

At that very moment I felt my blood pressure increase, "Is he under the impression that I'm not coordinated enough to hit a stupid little white ball in a field of grass?" I verbalized nothing but internalized everything, *"I'll show 'em! How hard can this be? I'm athletic. I work out. I'm confident in my ability to figure things out and adjust accordingly. I may not be the best, but I certainly won't be the worst."*

I asked him, "What type of clubs you got, Fred? Or are you playing with a dinosaur bone and a handful of gravel from Bedrock?"

Donnie let out an unfamiliar sigh. I knew he was waiting for me to crack a joke so that he could respond with one of his own, but surprisingly he didn't. He said his boss, *Mr. Slate*, gave him the day off and even if he had to start the car with his feet he wouldn't miss this one. Wow! No backlash from the Prince of Putdowns? This is huge. He is really making this out to be a big deal. I began to feel my level of excitement head north. Maybe it won't be so bad. Unlike the other sports where tenure is limited to a few years, I see eighty year old men playing golf.

Just as the light at the end of the tunnel began to shine, I heard Fred' s voice, "Tommy! Tommy! (my nickname from the television show, Martin, who has a job no one knows about) Are the proceeds from the charity event going to a good cause or going to you 'cause you're broke?" And before I could think of a comeback, he hung up.

All I could do was laugh. Our putdowns or wisecracks about each other are all in fun and each of us knows that when the chips are down we are there for each other with no questions asked. So to have Donnie hang up on me to get the last word in wasn't irritating at all. It was downright diabolical! And I knew that any attempt I made right then, whether it was a return call, an email or a text message, wouldn't suffice as the proper retribution so I just took one for the team and shook my head.

I had not heard from Marcus all day, and that was a little unusual. I mean, within a twenty-four hour time span I could speak to him five or six times. He and I have a lot of things in common. We both enjoy playing basketball and watching boxing matches. We both have outgoing personalities and are dreamers by nature. We see opportunities as finished products but have little interest in orchestrating the minor details to get there; and both of our wives complement our shortcomings as they really do serve as the *Yings* to our *Yangs.* I dialed his number and got his voicemail. I left him a message to call me to discuss the upcoming charity event, and before I could hang up he was chiming in on the other line.

"Wassup my boy, my boy, my boy, myyyyy boyyyyyyyyyy?"

That is the signature hello for Black Lalayne and we're all used to it.

"You in?" he asked.

"Uh, I guess so. Everybody seems to be excited about it. I just got off the phone with Frederico Head-a-rico and he is all amped up. Plus, Gazoo already booked us. Have you ever swung a club before?"

"No!" he replied, "But I am anxious to try. People say that it's a very addictive sport and once the bug crawls on you it takes over your soul."

"Now that was a good one," I said, "You sound like Vincent Price on MJ's "Thriller" album. If golf captures my soul and zombifies my existence then I have really underestimated my iron clad power of will. I WILL NOT make this into a habit. I WILL NOT let the golf bug crawl into my system and I most certainly WILL NOT spend thousands of dollars a year to play a game."

(As I sit here and write this passage I am laughing hysterically, because looking back at those comments I made demonstrates how naïve I was to the allure of the game of golf and how I was so wrong about my susceptibility to it!)

I ended the phone call with a sense of being content. I had made it abundantly clear that this "outing" would be for charity first, supporting our buddy second, and lastly…FUN with the fellas!

Chapter 2

Ready To Roll

"Wow! What a lovely morning!"

I rose from my bed and peered through the blinds of my bedroom window, eagerly wanting to put a visual to the lovely chirping sounds I heard from the other side of the glass. This was exactly why I moved to Florida! Suddenly, in a subtle but firm voice I hear, "Today is your big day, isn't it, Tigger?"

From the corner of my eye I thought I saw a puff of smoke and a witches broom as my wife entered the room. She was teasing me about the day that lay ahead of me. She knew that today was the day of the big charity event and wanted to get some sort of reaction from me so that she could gauge my level of enthusiasm.

"That's TIGER!" I replied, "Tigger is the character from Winnie the Pooh."

She looked at me, rolled her eyes, took a sip of her witches brew, then spoke as if she was about to have a house dropped on her.

"Relax! I was just joking with you! Did you wake up, roll out of bed and onto a cactus plant? Why don't you take a deep breath and release the tension in your butt cheeks!"

Maybe I was being a little short with her. I've been guilty of that crime before. She wouldn't have snapped back at me without a valid reason. As I went into the bathroom to take a shower and get ready for my day in the tree-less forest I reached back and gently released my pajamas from the grip of my buttocks.

I realized that I didn't have a clue what to wear. I'd never played golf before so I was unaware of the approved dress code. I've seen funny golf movies like *"Caddy Shack"* with Bill Murray and *"Easy Money"* with Rodney Dangerfield and Joe Pesci. Their outfits were far beyond my dress style so I decided to *"Youtube"* Tiger Woods to see what he was wearing. OK, red Nike cap...check; red Nike shirt...check; black shorts...hold on, its 90 degrees outside and I will not be wearing *anything* black today, and I am certainly NOT wearing any tight John Stockton shorts either. I gathered myself and pieced together an outfit that would allow me to retain my urban New York style and self esteem. While headed towards the front door, I strolled past a mirror and couldn't help thinking that my outfit made me look like a cross between Richie Cunningham of *"Happy Days"* and Ice Cube from *"Boyz In The Hood"*.

The initial plan was for us to meet at Steve's house and together we would storm the Event. As I exited the driveway my stomach began to rumble and howl as if it had a mind of its own. So, you know the drill. Illuminate the *"R"* on the dashboard, back the car into the driveway, run into the house, grab a magazine and pray no one is in the bathroom.

OK. Let's begin again.

On the drive to Steve's house my mind began flexing its ability to taunt, and I had to combat it by verbally reinforcing positive thoughts, *"Why am I so nervous? I don't even like golf. If I screw up; so be it. I won't ever see these folks again. This is just for fun; so being nervous and uptight is ridiculous. Today is a day to relax and chill with friends. You are not going to be judged or ridiculed in any way, so cool out. But what if everyone hits good shots and you look like a fool? What if someone recognizes you? What if your stomach decides that it's time for your booty to belch? "*

My mind and I were going through an exercise that occurs whenever I enter the realm of uncertainty. This familiar struggle is one I have been dealing with since childhood. Like the onset of a common cold, its symptoms are recognizable and unwelcome but there is little I can do to prevent it from occurring.

About forty five minutes later I arrive at Steve's house and he greets me with his Cheshire Cat grin.

"Wassup? You ready?"

"I'm ready," I replied, "What about a set of clubs? I don't have any."

"I got you!" he says, "I've got an extra pair of clubs that I used before I bought my new set. You can use them." From behind a set of worn tires in a dark corner of his garage, Steve fetches an old dusty duffel bag with an assortment of warped golf clubs inside. I look at them and instantly begin feeling like the *"Charlie Brown"* character, *Pig-Pen*. He then brings out the set he will be playing with – and it's a brand new red leather Nike cart bag with shiny new Nike clubs. My jaw dropped because I was familiar with the Nike brand and its *'Swoosh'* symbol, but I was unfamiliar with the brands I would be promoting that day. I had never heard of a Nitro Golf-X driver or a Ray Cook extreme aim putter. I did hear the name Ray Cook before. He was a legend in New York City sports. He was the guy responsible for monitoring the lights of the basketball court once the sun went down.

As I shook off the glazed look I was sporting I noticed that Steve's attire was a little different from mine. His non-fitting Nike cap matched his Nike Dri-Fit shirt which fell on top of his Nike golf pants.   Hmmm! I'm not the brightest bulb in the carton but clearly I missed something.

"Why didn't you tell me this was a fashion show?" I asked.

"What do you mean? I just grabbed something from the closet this morning. It's no big deal," he replied.

I gave him the alcoholic ass face. You know the face that a real alcoholic gives to you when he asks you to lend him money and you tell him you ain't got it. Just then Marcus speeds up into Steve's driveway.

"My boys, my boys, my boys, myyyyyy boyyyyyyyyys!"

He comes over and gives us both the customary handshake and man-hug then walks next door and rings the doorbell of Steve's neighbor. After a few hand gestures and wide smiles I see the neighbor's garage door rise. Marcus walks in and then comes out with a nice set of Ping Golf clubs and shoulder bag.

"What the….?"

Black Lalayne was in full effect. He had managed to finagle a set of excellent clubs from an exceptional golfer. Steve's neighbor was a scratch golfer. He and Marcus had struck up a conversation during the last sporting event that Steve had invited us to and which I'd been unable to attend. Marcus, or should I say Black Lalayne, made it clear that we were participating in a charity golf event and his clubs were outdated so Steve's neighbor offered to lend his clubs. As Marcus swung the bag around his right shoulder I noticed that the bottom of his shirt jumped out from the grip of his belt and shorts and migrated north of his navel.

"Aye! What size is that shirt? Infant? Or did you mistakenly put on the doll's clothes today? They must have had a sale going on in Smallville!" Cruel wisecrack, but necessary! See, either way I was the worst of the group. Remember, my clothes were sending mixed messages and my clubs needed to be bathed in WD40! I had to make a crack to set them back on their heels. If I was to let one start in on me without whipping my tongue first then they all would follow suit.

"Are we waiting on Fred?" asked Marcus.

Steve replied "He's gonna meet us there. He says it's easier for him to go straight there from his house; but you know he's gotta make an entrance!"

We all chuckle because we know our friend Donnie.

We packed our clubs in the trunk and jumped in the car to head out. I'm still wrestling with my internal voice as he has begun to open dialogue again.

"*You should have stayed home. Now you're gonna be out there in that heat sweating like you stole something and everyone is gonna be laughing at you. You didn't even dress the part.*" My stomach chimed in with a rumble and I put my hand on my gut as if it would subdue the noise.

We pulled into the parking lot, which was filled with luxury cars. Two Bentleys here, three or four Mercedes there and a couple Ferrari's lined our row. By this time my stomach was a raging well of water and rising steadily. I didn't want to be there. All of these folks are going to be just as I envisioned them. I'm going to stand out like a sore thumb on a foot. I hope we can just get to the carts undetected so that I can slip my sack of aluminum sticks on and disappear amongst the crowd before anyone notices. Just then I hear an old TuPac song roaring from a car stereo. I thought to myself. *"Who would be dumb enough to…"* Then I realized who was missing from the group. At the top of his lungs and from about fifty yards away we hear:

"Yo-Yo fellas! The champ is here!"

Well, so much for my disappearing act. Donnie drove right up to us and started in before he even parked.

"Oh hell to the no! Look at Black Nicholas with that toddler shirt buttoned all the way up to his esophagus! Oh, and his twin brother, Tiger Hood, with his Chicago Bulls colors on. We are on the green today not on the hardwood, baby! And why did y'all let grand-mamma come out looking so rusty with clubs from the Dollar Store. Where's our cart? Let's get this party started!"

We were all here now; and there was no turning back. The four amigos had finally crash-landed on the Golf Channel. I decided to man up and deal with the day as it would unfold. I kept telling myself, *"It's for a good cause and no one will care what you look like or how you played today. Plus this is a 'one and done' situation. After today you won't ever have to swing a golf club again. You can go back to doing what you do and enjoying the activities you are comfortable with. You are here as part of a support system and today is NOT about you!"*

We registered our group at the table and received our bag of goodies filled with items from the participating sponsors. Our golf bags were placed onto our carts and all the participants were making their last-minute preparations before heading to their respective chariots. I made one final dash to the restroom then grabbed some water on the way out to keep myself from becoming dehydrated. It was now two minutes before start time and the announcer was going over the rules of play. Black Lalayne and I occupied one cart and Fred Head and Gazoo in the other.

As the starter raised the fake pistol to begin the "Scramble" I said a quick prayer, hoping that everything would go well without any hiccups. I asked for a memorable day out with my friends and for the weather to remain well below ninety degrees.

"*POW!*" The loud shot signaled that the event was now underway and everyone began racing to their respective starting points. Just as Marcus mashed his foot on the pedal to move our cart, my bag slid off the back and onto the pavement, the clubs clanking together as if someone had dropped a bunch of fake nickels.

DAMN!!!

Chapter 3

Putt - Putt - Pass

We arrived at our team's designated starting point, which was hole number six. A scenic 154 yard PAR 3 with water running directly in front of the tee box, creating an island oasis feel. Fred jumped out of the cart first, followed by Gazoo, Black Lalayne then me. In my mind I was thinking it's about to go down. If you were an innocent by-stander watching our cinematic approach onto the tee box you would probably think we were filming the third installment of the classic movie, "*Hangover Part 3*".

"Who wants to lead the pack?" asked Steve.

"Let's get a hitting order for the day and strategize our play," said Donnie.

"Marcus, you tee off first, then Tommy, then Steve, and I'll go last. This way if you guys that haven't played before hit bad shots we will know to play it safe or go right at the pin." Sounded like a good strategy to me.

Marcus steps up to the tee box carrying his chosen club, an 8 iron. With his collar tucked down into the back of his "baby" blue shirt, he lines up his shot. He takes two slow practice swings and pauses at the end of his follow-through as if he just hit it and it's on the green already.

"What the hell are you doing?" yells Fred.

Marcus settles in and hits a nice shot and it's headed right at the pin…so we thought. As it crossed the water hazard, it continued over the green and into the street. We all yelled "DAMN!" simultaneously. Marcus was still in his follow-through pose when Fred asked, "What did you hit that with? An aluminum bat?" We all laughed and joked that Black Lalayne needed to chill with the steroids.

Now it's my turn at bat. I have never really swung a club before so the guys were suggesting a 5 or 6-iron to get me started. We'd taken a couple of practice swings in Steve's yard before we left and he'd shown me how I should try and grip it; but when you are faced with uncertainty you always resort to what you know and what feels comfortable. So I grab the 5 iron because I would rather be a little long than end up short and at the bottom of the lake. Marcus took two practice swings and his shot went towards the hole – so I'm gonna do the same.

"Whoosh!" Practice swing number one. I hit the ground and dug up some earthworms. The vibrations from the impact sent tingling sensations down my body to my extremities. *"OK, relax! You can do this! Take a step back and refocus."* I got back into position for another attempt and "Whoosh!" Practice swing number two just kissed the grass and felt much better than its predecessor. I've got it now. I can do this. I lined up my shot, gripped the club like it's the ninth inning of the World Series with two outs, took the club back until I tapped my right shoulder blade then swung it forward like a home run hit. "Whoosh!" I know I hit the ball, but I don't see it. I didn't hear or see any splash, so I know my ball didn't go in the water. Oh, maybe it's already in the hole. My level of excitement went through the roof. I'm thinking to myself, "I may be a natural". As I reached down with great anticipation to pick up my tee – "Abracadabra!" There's a bright white ball laying twelve inches in front of me. The guys are laughing hysterically! I, on the other hand, didn't see what was so funny. I was so focused and nervous that I didn't even think that it could be MY ball. I was in total denial. After a bit of persuasion from my teammates I accepted my fate and picked up *someone else's* golf ball.

Steve stepped up, and as he leaned over into his stance to take his practice swing, Donnie whispered to me, "Look at the size of that melon. It looks like he is off balance and gonna tip over any minute". As he swung the club forward, Steve's shot went airborne then took a little draw to the left. He landed right off the back side of the green and looked back at us as if to say, "I told you so". We were happy to have a ball somewhere near the green to putt, and congratulated him on his shot.

Donnie had to outdo Steve. (Yes, we were competing as a team but the old saying is definitely true. Whenever athletes, either past or present, get into any type of competitive situation their innate competitive spirit undoubtedly arises whether they want it to or not.) Like the star performer in a Broadway play who is about to perform his solo, Donnie begins his tee box ritual. He steps up in between the slanted posts and stares eagerly across the pond and directly at the pin. His demeanor is transformed from that of an erratic little school boy to a laser-like grad student about to negotiate his first pay raise. It seemed as if the pace of Donnie's ritual began to unfold in slow motion. We watched as he walked around the cart and selected a club from his bag, then approached the tee box with extreme confidence. He bent over to place his ball in position and then lined up into his stance. He brought the club back off the ball to approximately the height of his front right shoulder then propelled it downward onto the back of the ball. "Whoosh!" The ball took an awkward flight pattern as it went so far left that we thought he was about to be responsible for repairing someone's roof. But as we followed the flight path of the ball it began to fade back to the right and dropped right onto the green about three feet from the pin!

UNBELIEVABLE!

We all looked in amazement; as we were dazzled by what had just occurred. We began slapping high fives and celebrating his great shot. Donnie was still in his PGA pose. As he released his mental grip on fantasy he pumped his fist, yelled out, "Alright! Now follow the leader." Then he bent over to pick up his tee. While returning to a standing position I noticed something falling out of the front pocket his shirt. The unique object looked much like a small replica of a brontosaurus bone. He quickly picked it up from the uniform blades of manicured green grass and whispered, "My good luck charm!" before getting back into his cart.

What a character!!

What a Fred Head!!

As our carts maneuvered the cart path around the backside of the green I saw Donnie's ball lying motionless in the middle of the beautiful green landscape. From this angle we were able to look back at the tee box and truly admire his shot. As we exited our carts and approached the topside of the green I began inhaling the beauty of my surroundings and the perfection of the accompanying silence.

"Alright fellas, we have four chances to make this birdie putt!" said Steve, "Donnie, since you put us here you do the honors and take us home."

Donnie bent down to one knee to measure his putt. With a slight break moving from left to right and going downhill, this putt was not going to be straightforward. As he hovered over the ball I noticed that he was casting a mighty big shadow but I kept that wisecrack in my back pocket. Donnie struck the back of the ball with a light tap, sending it about two ball widths left and we watched as it slid downhill and just left of the cup.

"Awww, damn! I should have went straight at it!" he said.

"Don't you mean Yabba-Dabba Doo?" said Marcus. "Watch out, Fred. Let me put this in. This is all about touch."

Marcus bent his knees and leaned over his ball to putt. He ever so gently touched the back of his ball with his putter and we watched the ball roll right, break back left and then stop on the front side of the cup. He did a few jumping jacks to possibly get the last revolution out of the ball to make it drop in the hole, but it had run out of gas.

Steve jumped in front of me to putt. He believed that he could save the day. He took another look at how the break towards the hole was, then lined up his ball. He bent over to putt and went straight at the hole. It rimmed around the outside and swung the ball right. *"Another failed putt,"* I thought.

"OK, Tommy. You are the last shot! Take your time and follow the line. You saw how it breaks, stay in between their lines and you'll be fine."

I stepped up ready and filled with excitement. I can make this putt. I've played miniature golf since I was a child and putting is something I felt confident with. I bent down to view the line. I lined up my ball one ball length outside the left end of the cup. I stepped over the ball and bent into my putting stance. Just then two tournament Rangers were riding towards us and stopped to allow me the courtesy of making my putt in silence. Now, with the added pressure of more people watching and the re-

26

emergence of my gut conversation, I cautiously moved my putter away from my ball and decided to take a few practice strokes. I lifted my head to make a comment that would lessen the tension of the situation and my lack of concentration caused my second practice stroke to strike the ball sending it down the hill and off the green.

"…..Aaaaaaaaaaaand I guess that is PAR for you guys," said the Ranger. "Pressure not only bursts pipes, it tightens asses too!"

I was mortified and disgusted because I could have made that putt. If they hadn't distracted me I would have been able to focus in and lift my team to victory. Up until then I was a bit optimistic. Now I was feeling the increasing buildup of frustration. I picked up my ball and got back into the cart. No one said a word but I could sense a bit of disappointment.

"No problem. That was just the first hole. We just got to warm up a bit," said Steve.

I appreciated the way he tried to ease the frustration and anxiety I was experiencing; but oddly enough I was looking forward to the next hole.

As we muddled through the next few holes we began to see a pattern unfold. Each member of the group began to focus in on what we were trying to accomplish together and we took advantage of our strengths. Donnie was our clean-up guy. Steve's chipping and putting was a huge asset and the powerful swings of Marcus' clubs kept a slight breeze on our faces. My contributions showed up every so often when the cart girl rounded our position and I was able to flag her down to get us all a cold drink.

As the day progressed we made our way to hole fourteen. There we noticed a group of people awaiting our arrival. Hole fourteen was another gorgeous PAR three with water on the right and a very sandy bunker on the left side of the green. In front of the tee box was a wide moat in which many brand new golf balls had decided to take refuge. Staring at the green 195 yards downwind, it seemed a bit overwhelming to me; but we prepared to do battle.

As we exited our cart the waiting people explained that they were issuing a 'Closest to the pin' challenge and for a $5 donation, should you succeed, the prize would be a quart of rum.

"Oh hell, yeah. I'm gonna pay for Marcus to do this with his sand wedge!" yells Donnie. He puts a five dollar bill into the hand of the hole-monitor and we all chuckle as the uncertainty of using a sand wedge for a 195 yard strike is reflected on Marcus' face.

"Never mind him. He's just kidding!" said Steve.

Marcus grabbed his 6 iron. With the wind at his back he approached the tee box with something to prove. Donnie had paid for him to enter the 'Closest to the pin' contest but in actuality he knew it was another one of

Fred's attempts to prank him. He tried to remain calm and focus on his shot but I believe he wanted it too much. He swung his club a little too hard and overshot the green again; and of course Donnie chimed in with, "Told you to use the pitching wedge."

I decided to jump onto the tee box with the 3 wood I pried from my sack. It was a little worn, with strong scuff marks grooved into the club face, but it was the one club I had yet to swing. I had nothing to lose because no one expected anything from me except another lost ball. I gripped the club hard and swung for the upper deck. The club hit the ball from the tee box and drove it straight across the moat, in between the water and sand bunker and it rolled right onto the green. Everyone looked on in amazement. It was my first decent hit of the day. Of course I was surprised too, but somehow I remained poker-faced. As I reached down to take my tee from the ground I said a little "Thank you" to the man upstairs. After so many disappointments I have to admit that the congratulations I received for that shot felt gratifying. I did not win the rum but what I gained was a sense of accomplishment.

Now I wanted more. I wanted to hit that same shot again and again. I did it once; which meant I could do it again. I began searching my mental Rolodex for the feeling and movements of that last shot.

"Did I follow through? Am I keeping my head down? Maybe I should be hitting the 3 wood all the time?"

With my excitement bubbling on the inside and my desperate attempt to keep my cool, one thing I knew for certain…I was most definitely making my deodorant work overtime.

As the day progressed, so did my ball strikes. They didn't all go straight nor did they all end up miles down the fairway. I was all over the course. I hit trees, yardage markers and other fairways. Heck, I even scared an alligator! I was happy just to be making consistent contact with the ball. I was happy to see the ball fly forward for a change. Straightening it up was something that would come later.

When we arrived at the final hole of the day the hitting order was in total disarray. I wanted to hit that ball and hit it as hard and as far as possible. I wanted to outdo everyone. Hole number five was a dogleg left, 525 yard PAR 5 with a huge fairway. No immediate obstacles in sight, so we could just let her rip. Everyone grabbed their drivers from their bags. Me? I chose my trusty old 3 wood.

Steve looked at me and said, "Come on and hit your driver. You're going to need to get more distance than what the 3 wood can give you."

I was reluctant to do so, but since it was team play I had to do what was best for our team as a unit. I walked back to the sack on my cart. I placed the 3 wood into the darkness of that potato bag then freed the driver from its lair. It felt a little heavier and the difference in the size of the club head was quite noticeable. In my rational mind it made sense to go with a bigger, sturdier club. I swung the club with all the erroneous technique I had acquired over the last seventeen holes. I was feeling comfortable and a bit confident. As long as I made contact I should be fine. I was in a groove and it was showing in my demeanor. The earlier gastro-conversations were a thing of the past. My look at the three amigos was not one of fear or disdain. It was more along the lines of, "Where should I target? Should I stay left of the bunker on the left or go over it?"

I lined up my shot and took the familiar practice swings. I gripped the club, cocked it back and released it like a medieval sledgehammer. The ball took off from the tee and disappeared in flight. Wow! That felt amazing! It's like the ball exploded on impact. Everyone heard the hit; and now it's time to find the evidence.

We all jumped into our carts and raced down the fairway. We slowed down at roughly 200 yards. Nothing. We continued out to about 230 yards. Nothing. Wow! I must have really crushed it. We checked the sand bunker, but no luck. We came up on one ball lying outside the front side of the bunker. It's a Titleist.

"That's me!" yelled Donnie. Ten yards ahead we find another ball. This one's a Nike. "That must be me," said Steve. Marcus and I were still in search mode. Directly across the fairway from Steve's ball was a bright orange ball which belonged to Marcus.

"I guess you can just drop where I am," he said. "I thought I hit that one good," I said. "Yeah, me too, but we all lost it in flight. No worries. We've still got good second shots."

We all gathered around Marcus' shot. He was lying on the left side of the fairway just into the bend. With roughly 285 yards remaining, we started to strategize on how to score a birdie. Our plan was to hit shots inside 100 yards and then a third shot onto the green close to the pin. Marcus pulled out his trusty 6 iron which we nicknamed "Ole Reliable". He hit a shot about 200 yards but it went right and into the woods. Donnie hit his famous left to right shot and he too went into the woods. Steve flubbed his shot by picking his head up too fast and his shot was straight but only went about 50 yards. Because of the narrow fairway and only one ball remaining, I decided to drop my ball up ahead where Steve flubbed his so that if I miss-hit I would be able to retrieve it.

On our way up to Steve's ball Marcus drove over a bump and the back tires kicked up some debris. Donnie yelled for us to stop. As we came to a halt we noticed a ball lying smack in the middle of the fairway. Could this be…? Nah, it couldn't be. A closer look revealed a familiar red dot on the back and when I picked it up it read 'Bridgestone'! "This IS my ball!" Somehow the golf gods must have maneuvered my ball through the trees and placed it into the bend of the manicured fairway.

With the new-found evidence we made an executive decision to hit again from the location of my ball. Since I hit the best drive I felt I had earned the honors. With the excitement of hitting such a marvelous drive pounding through the fibers of my Polo shirt I felt certain that I could hit another shot to get us close to the green. My confidence was swelling and in my mind I was getting the hang of this golf thing. Who knows, I could be a natural and pick it up very quickly. If I put my mind to it I could have this mastered in a few days.

I grabbed my 3 wood and eyed the wide green. Sitting about 250 yards from the pin our strategy was to hit a shot inside of 50 yards or reach the pin, if possible. I bent my knees, kept my head down with eyes focused on my ball. I took the club back behind my head and turned my whole body so that I could get more distance on impact. I brought the club downward from behind my head with enormous speed and strength…PANG!!!!!!

I made connection with the back of the ball then picked my head up to see it in its beautiful flight through the aqua blue sky. As I was searching the clouds for my ball I caught a glimpse of a black and yellow flying object. For a moment it startled me, as I thought I had witnessed a UFO sighting, but then realized that I'd hit the ground before impacting the ball, snapping the club head from its shaft and propelling it further than the ball.

What the…..?????

Chapter 4

The Aftermath

The very next morning I was sore. My right clavicle was experiencing a nagging pain as if I'd been beaten mercilessly with a blunt object. My radius and ulna bones found themselves at war with their neighboring nerve endings and I couldn't get my thumb to hug his four siblings and make a fist. My body was a mess. I lumbered out of bed and made my way to the medicine cabinet. I yelled out to my wife, "What is the strongest medication we have in the house for pain?"

She replied, "Midol!"

I was definitely NOT in a joking mood. I needed relief. She quickly gathered two pain pills and a glass of water for me.

"Here, take these. It will ease the pain a little."

I swallowed those pills as if I was Pac-Man eating a bunch of power pellets. I really didn't expect the pills to work. I took them because I believed my mind needed a stimulant that would force my body's natural healing powers to react on their own and dull my sensitivity to the pain.

Mind over matter?

Whatever!!!!!

I laid back down to rest my aching body only to hear the phone ring. I had no intention of picking it up, even though it was within an arm's length, and since voicemail is included in our bundled cable subscription I was certain our 24 hour electronic employee was working her shift. Moments later I hear chuckles and giggles along with, "…I don't know if he still wants to go. He's playing the invalid role today…"

Playing??? I certainly wasn't *playing* anything today.

Constantly tossing and turning in an attempt to find the most comfortable position to rest in I found myself replaying the events that occurred the day before. From the initial spark of the starter pistol to the UFO sighting, I went over what I thought I could have changed or done better.

"Maybe if I didn't swing so hard on a couple of those chip shots? What if I would have tried to play below the pin as opposed to hitting past it and putting mostly downhill? Would it have helped me be more effective? What if I took a lesson or two?"

"HOLD THE PHONE!!!!!!"

"Why am I thinking about this? Golf is not my sport, and yesterday's outing was a one-time event. Sure, we had a blast, but we always have a blast together. I know I am a

very competitive person and I hate to lose; but this doesn't count. I was doing this as a favor for a friend." I knew that I had to verbalize my thoughts so that my mind could hear the rational voice and direct my heart to open its doors and free itself. I bowed out from the conversation and took a nap. Who knew that Midol would not only ease aches and pains….it's a sleep aid too.

A few hours later I rose from my slumber, showered, grabbed a bite to eat and headed out the door. It was about 4:30pm, and tip off for my basketball league game was at 7pm. I headed down to the mall to buy a new pair of sneakers, as my old pair had developed a wide-mouth smile in the front. At the entrance to the store I picked up the daily flyer that highlights all of the active specials and discount coupons. I asked the salesperson for the whereabouts of the men's athletic footwear and she replied, "Sir, it's towards the back of the store on your right. Look for the PGA display and directly behind it you'll find what you're looking for." I gently nodded a "Thank you" to her and began my quest for the PGA display.

With time running short I adjusted the pace of my steps and began walking with a sense of urgency.   I passed rows of bicycles, clothing and camping equipment and to tell the truth I had no idea what a 'PGA' was. I continued my pace looking down each row on my right as if I was playing hide and seek. I stumbled onto some men's running shoes and then some colorful new Nike cross trainers with a style I had never seen before. I paused and picked up a pair to feel their weight and I noticed some type of prickly objects on the bottom. *"Perhaps these are a new type of cleat,"* I thought. I looked over my left shoulder and I saw Tiger Woods in full swing with the PGA logo alongside his poster. My extraordinary sense of conclusion created a doubt that maybe these were NOT cleats and I bet PGA had something to do with golf!

DUH!

I tried on a pair of the new Tiger Woods' shoes just for fun. They were OK, but too costly for me. I shook my head because I wouldn't spend $100 for a pair of shoes that didn't make me jump higher or run faster; but I wanted to see if I looked good in them. I found a mirror, grabbed one of the display irons and started taking slow motion swings. I reached up and put on the Nike TW cap to complete the look. I must say, the look was good and I felt even better. After about ten swings I began to dismantle my costume. I was beginning to attract attention. Unaware that there was another patron behind me watching my swing, I heard, "Hey buddy, what's your handicap?"

HANDICAP???

Did this little four-foot-tall munchkin just ask me if I was handicapped? How insanely rude of him! I looked at him with the annoyed alcoholic ass face, released the baseball grip I had on the display club (as I didn't want to catch an assault case) and abruptly darted over to the athletic footwear section. I quickly came across a pair of *"magical"* Jordan shoes that would make me play like Bow Wow. I hurried to the front, purchased them for $99.99 and left the store. Before I started the car I thought to myself, *"I bet that little rude guy in the store must be one of those stuffy folks. You know, the Perrier-drinking, dollar-bill sweat-wiping, big car driving type."* In my car I sat back and enjoyed a laugh at the expense of the little guy, but shame on me for prejudging another. I put the key in the ignition and drove away from the building. Just before I exited the parking lot I saw an extended cab Cadillac Escalade ESV on what seemed to be 24 inch rims… and the driver's seat was against the steering wheel.

HMMM!

Chapter 5

Pandora's Box

After the game, Marcus, Steve, Donnie and I decided to stop off as we always do and eat some wings. We talked about the events that occurred during the game and laughed at how Donnie resembled a "pig in a blanket" because his uniform was so tight. He had a great game, scoring eighteen points by knocking down six 3-point shots. He made sure we recognized his accomplishments, and being ever so slick-witted he replied, "Yeah, I shoot better with my hooves on".

We continued laughing and joking and somehow our conversation turned to the charity golf event.

"I think we were robbed with a starter pistol," said Marcus.

"Robbed?" said Steve.

"Yeah! Robbed! We should have won something. Maybe not from the scorecard but surely a Best or Worst Dressed, a Most Likely To Harm The Wildlife or Most Disruptive Group Ever To Swing A Club!"

I raised my hand. "Yep! Worst dressed was definitely me. Hands down I would have won that trophy!"

"Luckily Steve and I played decent or we would have been really screwed!" said Donnie.

"What do you mean by that?" I said.

Everyone sat up. Something was brewing and the lid of Pandora's Box had been opened. If that question had been sidestepped or omitted then the following events would not have occurred. But with the four of us plus our competitive spirit constantly on the prowl, the tight 4-man group is always shadowed by a potential fifth Beatle.

Donnie proceeded to answer, "What do I mean? Were you blind to the fact that for every shot or putt that you and Marcus screwed up, either Steve or I came to the rescue? I was beginning to think that you guys forgot that the object of the game was to put the ball in the hole with the LEAST number of strokes. Not the MOST! "

DING! DING! DING! The bell signaling hurt pride had been rung.

"So let me get this straight. You think we couldn't have done it without y'all? I believe that, in a team format, Marcus and I could definitely give you two a run for your money!" I replied.

"You must be drunk," said Donnie.

"I'm serious! I don't think that you and Steve would beat us as bad as you think. Heck, you stand a good chance of losing!" I said. Donnie and Steve just laughed.

"Check please. I think our buddy has had one too many!" said Steve.

"I bet that Marcus and I could beat Fred and Gazoo in a game and if we didn't win we would not be more than 5 strokes behind!" I challenged. I guess Steve and Donnie, and probably Marcus too, thought I was being facetious.

"That is NOT even a bet I would take for the money; but for bragging rights we'll do it!" said Steve.

"Whenever!!! However!!!" I strongly suggested.

On the way home my spider-senses were tingling. Unfortunately they were about an hour too late because I had already put myself in a compromising situation; and to top it off I'd dragged Marcus in without getting his approval. I knew I couldn't retract my challenge because of my enormous pride but I had little confidence in our ability to come out on top. I didn't own any golf clubs or golf attire. I didn't know the rules (nor do I care to), and did Marcus even want to play with me? See, if we were to lose this challenge we would give the other two guys enough ammunition to use against us FOREVER! I asked myself, "*WHY*? *Why did I open my mouth?*" Suddenly my stomach decided to answer for me; and fortunately for me I was close enough to pull into the driveway, run into the house, grab a magazine and pray that no one was sitting on the throne.

The following day I get a call from Marcus; and to my surprise he is eagerly up for the challenge.

"I think we can beat them," he said.

That was definitely a sigh of relief for me. So now all I had to do was set the date. Well, that wasn't exactly *all* I had to do. I also needed to get my own set of clubs. I needed appropriate golf attire and I needed to practice so that I could hit the ball towards the hole consistently instead of out of bounds or into the street. We all agreed to play a round two weeks later. It will be *Fred-Head* and *Gazoo* versus *Black Lalayne* and *Tommy*. The winners get lifelong bragging rights.

I immediately went shopping for proper golf attire; I refused to subject myself to another day of hip-hop golf. Since Nike was the brand I was most familiar with I proceeded to pick up a couple of shirts, shorts and a pair of shoes. After my wardrobe was upgraded I then focused my attention on a set of clubs. I bought the Nike Sasquatch Driver and Slingshot Irons. I figured Phil Knight would be proud of me. I was feeling good about myself. I set up a little swing area in the backyard of the house and a putting station in the garage with a machine I received as a gift at a Christmas party some years ago.

As the saying goes, '*Practice makes perfect*'... but actually I learned that '*Perfect practice makes perfect*'. If you practice something new and you start with bad habits then you reinforce the bad habits with every practice.

Makes sense, doesn't it? Well, it didn't to me at that moment. My focus was on winning. I honestly thought that my baseball grip and over the shoulder swing coupled with a front leg and head lift would get me to where I was going.

As I began my practice sessions in the back yard the first 20 balls I hit across the pond went right – hard right! I was becoming extremely frustrated. My common sense told me to turn my body and aim left. By doing so, my shot should fall in the middle of the fairway. I tried it and the more balls I hit the more I thought I'd bought some defective balls. I decided to put the driver down and go putt. Putting was the most comfortable part of the game for me. I had played putt-putt (miniature) golf before and had done well, so this was something I felt comfortable with. I putted about 20 balls and sank roughly half of them. I was on! My putting was OK! I didn't really need putting practice. I needed to find a way to hit that little white dimpled ball onto the fairway and up to the hole in four strokes or less.

Instead of taking lessons, (an idea which had crossed my mind), I decided to get free instruction from "YouTube". I typed *G-O-L-F-S-W-I-N-G* into the search field and I found a video that showed NBA Hall of Famer Charles Barkley playing golf. I decided to click on it because of his connection to the game of basketball and I thought maybe I could learn something, as I know Charles has famous golf buddies. What I witnessed was pure horror. Charles looked as if he was being remotely controlled by a kid, and his batteries had run out! He had the worst swing I could have imagined. I figured he was joking because we all know Charles as being a "personality" and this most certainly had to be a gimmick. But as I witnessed more and more videos of Charles' swing I quickly learned what NOT to do. I laughed hysterically until my abdominal muscles were on fire. I would like to say, "Thank you, Charles for providing a lot of entertainment and even a bit of *edutainment*. You definitely taught me the importance of being able to laugh at myself."

Marcus called me to make sure I was still focused on the task at hand. He knew that I absolutely did not want to lose to Steve and Donnie. He asked how I was coming along with my practice sessions. I said it was a work in progress and invited him to come to the house to putt a few. About fifteen minutes later I heard a car in my driveway.

"Wassup Dude? You know we are gonna beat them, right?"

I replied "Certainly! It'd be a sin to lose to them." I opened up the garage door and exposed my makeshift putting green. We each took turns putting and strategizing for our upcoming challenge.

"Do you think they are practicing?" he said.

"I don't know. I believe that they think we'll fold under the pressure. As long as we stay focused on what we're trying to do and try *not* to hit two bad shots back to back, we should be fine," I said.

Two weeks later the four of us met at a beautiful public course near the west central Florida coastline. Fred and Gazoo rode in together. The smirks on their faces annoyed me a bit. I almost could hear what they were thinking. I put on my game face and unloaded my new clubs onto our cart.

"Woo-Hoo! Look at Tommy! New clubs, new clothes and new shoes…he went school shopping! Too bad he got the same old game!" said Donnie.

"Laugh it up, pregnant neck! You just make sure you bring your "A" game today!" I replied.

We paid our fees at the golf shop and headed towards the first hole. The starter met us halfway and explained to us that they had a tournament going on today and play might be slow.

On the tee box for hole number one the four of us stood looking out onto the fairway. The wind was blowing slightly from left to right and the cool mist from the sprinkler system was tickling my cheekbones. Something about today felt special. I didn't feel any pressure at all. I felt calm and my stomach was asleep for once. We went over the rules of play for the day and tossed a quarter into the air to see what order we would play in. Heads we lead, tails we follow. As the bright silver coin rotated into the air and fell cautiously onto the blades of grass I could see George's face staring back at me and for a second I believed he winked an eye at me.

Marcus and I led off with nice shots onto the right side of the fairway. Our competitors followed. We both got onto the green with our second shots and putted twice for PAR. I was feeling good about our chances from here. Marcus and I kept whispering to each other to remain focused. As time went on we fell behind a few strokes but didn't panic. We maintained a steady pace and hit some very nice shots in the process. As we tried to mount a ferocious comeback the bad guys seemed to always have an answer. Even when they hit bad shots it seemed as though they always recovered well.

Throughout the day I noticed that Donnie would consistently bend over to identify his ball, then reach down and pick it up to clean it off. He didn't do it after every hit, only the ones off the fairway. What I realized later was that he never put it back down in the same place. I didn't say anything at first because we were often on opposite sides of the fairway. But leave it to Donnie to push the envelope. The last straw was when he completely moved his ball from behind a tree and into a clearing for a shot at the green. I stood on the other side of the fairway with my hands raised and watched him as if I was watching a robbery happen in slow motion. Funny thing was that he didn't think twice about it, nor did he try to hide it; and Steve just followed along.

"What's wrong?" Donnie yelled.

"What's wrong?? What's wrong?? I saw you move that ball position so you could get a good hit," I said.

"No I didn't. I was cleaning it off so that the debris wouldn't slow its flight!" he replied. I immediately cut my eyes at Steve and he quickly turned his head so that we wouldn't make eye contact. From past experience I knew that that was a copout so that he could say he didn't see it.

Yeah right!

Needless to say after 18 holes of golf Marcus and I came in a close second but to this day we all know that win has an asterisk next to it. Fred Head knows the truth. Gazoo watched it happen all day. We assumed their continuous laughter was due to having a good time, but maybe they had been getting away with murder the whole time. Maybe George's wink to me was a warning for us to play with one eye open at all times. Keep your eyes on the prize but don't forget to activate your peripheral vision when Fred Head and Gazoo are competing against you.

Lesson learned!

Chapter 6

Friend or Foe?

Whoever came up with the idea of working nine to five for a living surely didn't think about me during their brainstorming session. The standard equation of five days on versus two days off then repeat, does NOT equal happiness. At least NOT in my book. Life had begun throwing sharp uppercuts to my midsection and I had no defense for her persistent assault. Sore knees, swollen ankles, headaches and other achy body parts were all tell-tale signs of the need for some rest and relaxation.

But how can you truly rest when you have boxed yourself into a job where management overwhelms you by eliminating staff to directly influence their bottom line numbers and co-workers sell their souls to keep their jobs then stab you in the back whenever they feel threatened? And what about the hungry mouths at home who are dependent upon you for food, shelter and clothing, and are unaware of the debilitating time spent in the daily pressure cooker?

The basketball court used to be my safe haven. I used to be able to drown out the outside world and focus when in between the lines of the ninety-four-foot parallelogram. But the past few years have decreased my time to play and increased my commitment to work. I was becoming what I always said I would not be….a workaholic!

It is a known fact that stress can kill; and I was feeling the monkey on my back. Months had passed since I last hung out with the fellas, shot a basketball or even cracked a smile. I was becoming a hermit like my father and time was slipping by at warp speed. I knew I needed to do something but I was too tired and didn't know where to begin. I wanted to play basketball again because of the camaraderie and competition, but the allure wasn't as strong as it once had been. One evening, at the request of an old teammate, I got dressed to play, drove to the gymnasium but once there I couldn't muster up enough "*umph*" to get out of my car. I was physically and emotionally drained. My mental fortitude was gone.

About three months later I got a call from my employer regarding a large prospective client they had been targeting, "We really need for you to host a very prominent client of ours. He has an extremely reserved demeanor and this is his first visit to America. Maybe you can take him to do a Disney tour and introduce him to Mickey Mouse."

Reluctantly, I agreed to assume the role of the company's resident tour guide,

"*Keep your eyes on the big picture. Take one for the team. This may have promotion written all over it.*" I had to speak to the dark side of my emotional self. *His* take was not that of being a cooperative teammate. He believed that this was yet another situation where work had consumed our personal space; and he was unhappy, to say the least.

From the initial description of my guest it seemed he would be someone who would like to visit museums, view national landmarks and carry a huge zoom lens camera. I thought to myself, "*Maybe he wears a corduroy jacket with patches on the elbows, progressive bi-focal glasses and smokes hand rolled cigars.*"

When Mr. Lenwood appeared from the darkness of the airport tunnel I immediately noticed why I had been selected to play host. He walked directly up to me and said, "Hello, I'm Ronald Lenwood."

He extended his right hand for me to shake and when I reciprocated he grabbed me and gave me the friendly homeboy hug. I was totally in a space that left me a little off balance. I was stunned. I had assumed that I would be meeting a gentleman who was about the same age as my father and who probably lived in Mr. Roger's neighborhood. Conversely, I met a man who was not only lively and full of spunk; he probably hung out watching MTV. Well, you know what they say when you assume things.....

Ronnie, as he instructed me to call him, wanted to do everything in one day. He was energized and operating as if he was on borrowed time. "What's poppin' my man? What do you do for fun in this town?"

I still had a look of awe on my face and my jaw was stuck in its elongated position. I had questions but didn't know where to begin.

"How did you know who I was?" I asked. "Your perked-up eyes and office-like demeanor told me you were expecting someone; and I guessed correctly," he replied.

He asked me again, "What is there to do in this town for fun? When are we going to South Beach?"

I was at odds because I was trying to keep things as professional as possible without being viewed as a stiff-collared square, "Miami is approximately a four hour drive from here. Orlando is more feasible and only about an hour away. I thought we would go there and you could see Disney World."

Ronnie looked at me as if I was speaking a foreign language.

"Disney World? Really?" His sarcasm was surprising but inoffensive. He continued, "I'm sorry. You must be confused. I'm Ronald Lenwood Jr. I see you didn't get a copy of the memo. My father, Ronald Sr., was unable to make the trip because of unexpected health issues so I came as his replacement."

Ronnie could see my brain working to connect the dots. He needed to let me know that he was much different from his father. I read a lot more into it; I realized that

Ronnie wanted to enjoy the Florida nightlife and not socialize in the day with Mickey. In Florida, hand rolled cigars are a commodity and the process of their creation, an art form. I'm sure Mr. Lenwood Sr. would have enjoyed witnessing it; but to Junior it would probably be as much fun as watching paint dry. I immediately had to revamp my plans.

"Ronnie, let's get you squared away at your hotel first. From there we can decide what to do for dinner and beyond. I actually know of a great place downtown called The Luxury Box. A friend of mine owns the place and he is well connected. He also can give us some direction on good entertainment. How does that sound?"

He replied, "Now we're talking!"

I dropped Ronnie at the hotel to give him time to unpack and shake the cobwebs off from his long flight. I figured dinner and a few drinks would knock him out and we would start fresh tomorrow. When I returned to pick up my guest for dinner I noticed he was wearing a black cap with the TW insignia.

"I take it you're a Tiger Woods fan, eh?"

"Yep. Sure am! Do you play?"

"I dabble a bit. Actually I am just learning. It's been a while since I last swung my clubs but I really enjoy the peace and quiet when I'm out there."

"Did you just say 'peace and quiet'? How old are you? I can see why you were picked to host my father."

We both chuckled out loud and continued talking about sports; in particular, our golf games. During our drive to the restaurant I learned that Ronnie had been an avid golfer since the age of 15. He told me that many of his biggest business deals had been formulated on the golf course.

He said, "It's been my experience that the business proposal occurs between holes 3 and 7. The show of interest happens during the transition from front 9 to back 9. Between holes 11 and 14 the two parties are negotiating price and the closing ends with the customary handshake after the last putt is in the hole."

I found that statement to be very interesting. I didn't get the feeling that Ronnie was leading me astray. He said those words with such a nonchalant mien that there HAD to be some substance to them. Add to the fact that the Lenwood family were multi-millionaires, while I was a budding "thousand-aire" and what would Ronnie gain by selling me a dream? I was becoming more interested in my passenger's thought processes and experiences. I found it extremely interesting how we were in the same age group with similarities in our physical stature; but the main difference between us came down to approximately six inches less below his Nike cap and a few more zeros in his bank account.

After dinner we decided to have a few more drinks and watch the basketball game at the bar. Ronnie nabbed a barstool opening and I stood in the background directing the bartender to switch the channel. I leaned in to put my drink on the paper coaster and while returning to my original upright position I glanced down and noticed that Ronnie's feet were dangling three inches from the floor. I quickly turned my head before I let out a chuckle and immediately made eye contact with another friend who was at the bar. His name was Victor Crawley… and I wasn't in the mood for his shenanigans tonight; but it was too late. He was already en route.

"Wassup man? How ya doin? Haven't seen you in a while. What have you been up to?"

Victor was the neighborhood storyteller. We nicked named him "Juan Upman". You see, he was the kind of person who had experienced everything that could ever be labeled an experience and whatever story you narrated to a friend or group, he would always *one-up* you with a similar but more elaborate tale.

"Hey Vic! How are you tonight?" I replied.

"I'm awesome big fella! Awesome!" he said.

"My friend Ronnie and I just came in for a bite to eat and a few beers. He is in town for a few days on business and I'm his resident tour guide."

Ronnie extended his arm to Victor and the guys shook hands. Victor asked Ronnie where home was and when he responded, "Ireland", that's when Victor went in. "Ireland is a great country! Filled with beautiful women and the greenest golf courses you'll ever see. When I toured the amateur circuit with Tiger, we were invited to play at the Royal County Down in New Castle. He was a bit nervous but I told him to play with confidence. I finished 4 under and Tiger struggled to finish even PAR. Look at him now. I'm glad I was able to give some helpful advice to an up-and-coming star."

It took everything I had inside not to blast Victor for bending the truth but Ronnie found it entertaining. I rolled my eyes and turned my head towards the television set which was now showing the NBA highlights. Victor was still going on about his Ireland connections, asking Ronnie if he knew this person or that person. I watched Ronnie shake his head "No" repeatedly. Of course he wouldn't know the people Victor was asking him about. How could he? Victor most likely created them as he always does. A short while later Ronnie explained that Victor was scheduled to play a round of golf tomorrow with a friend and had invited us along to make it a foursome. I was very reluctant to accept; but my alternative was Mickey Mouse and Goofy! It also helped me have an excuse to cut the night short with Ronnie as the upcoming tee time was 8am. I dropped Ronnie back at his hotel room and headed home.

On the tee box the next morning, Ronnie, Victor, his friend Paul and I tossed a coin in the air to determine hitting order. As the coin rotated repeatedly in the air I got a flashback of George and his wink of warning. I smiled as the coin fell onto the ground. I was anxiously awaiting a similar sign from his copper cousin but I guess Mr. Lincoln chose to remain subdued. No wink meant no worries; so today I was going to immerse myself in the fun and enjoy myself. Paul led the way with a nice drive down the right side of the fairway. Ronnie followed and Victor and I rolled into the left side bunker. PAR-PAR-Double Bogey- and a pick up is how we began our day.

At the turn I noticed that Paul and Ronnie were continuously complimenting each other's shots and giving pointers to the less fortunate duo of Victor and me.

"I thought you could play?" I asked Victor, "You told that man you played against Tiger and gave him advice on how to get better. You lied, didn't you?"

"No, I didn't lie," Victor replied, "It was a long time ago; and I am just as guilty as the next man of giving advice and not following it. That is probably why I am not on tour now!" I cut my eyes at Victor. Even when caught in a lie Mr. Juan Upman wouldn't own up to it. He just continued to reconfigure all of the bunkers on the course by whacking sand onto the fairways.

On the final hole, Paul issued a bold challenge, "Guys, we are all within a similar putting range. Let's make it interesting. The first two to sink their putts will have lunch paid for by the remaining two. Are you guys in?"

Of course we were in. How could we say "No", even if we wanted to? The levels of testosterone on that green went from excessive to gi-normous! Ronnie missed his putt and so did Paul. Victor putted his ball on target but a bit too hard, as it rolled right over the hole and rested on the other side. At that time I was unaware of the etiquette of golf so I didn't wait for Victor to spot his ball. While he was jumping around and hissing at his misfortune, I lined up my ball and putted it downhill towards the 4.25 inch diameter cup. I squinted my eyes and maneuvered my body as if I had a WII controller in my hand. Down the hill it sailed and just over the cup went my putt, but luckily for me, Victor was still running his mouth and didn't pick his ball up in time – which allowed my ball to collide with his and bounce backwards into the hole!

After a brief debate I was finally declared the official winner of the challenge and we all shook hands. I noticed Ronnie's demeanor with Paul and in my mind I replayed some of their interaction during our round. I couldn't help but recall the golf blueprint that Ronnie had laid out for me and wondered if he had just closed another business deal right under my nose. I began to view the game from a different perspective. Many of my sophisticated peers were involved in this worldly culture; and I have to admit that I do enjoy myself when I play.

What am I missing by ignoring the recurring invites into "*Bogeyland*"?

At that very moment I made a promise to myself. From this day forward I would continue to broaden my horizons and embrace opportunities to create new experiences. I made a self-commitment to expand my circle of friends and reintroduce the concept of fun into my life. So I picked up my ball, dusted off the brown dirt that tried to attach itself to a winner and shouted, "Gentlemen, what's my limit for lunch?"

Chapter 7

In-Dependence

"I'm checking the site now to see what deals are available for Saturday!"

I was on the phone with a fellow golfer coordinating my weekly outing. I had started to play a round every week but still refused to take a lesson. Not that I was being cheap, but I was strongly convinced that once I took a professional lesson the game of golf would go from the arena of relaxation to that of sheer competition. It had happened with basketball and I was trying to alleviate stress, not increase it.

"Tee time is 9am. Please let the guys know and I will see you Saturday morning!"

I returned the receiver to its base. I reached in my pocket and unraveled a coupon I had extracted from the local newspaper. There was a two-day sale on Nike golf balls and I was not going to play with the ones I had anymore. The ones that lived in my golf bag were battered and abused to the point where they needed to be laid to rest. Some were warped. Some were tanned. Some had extra dimples and some weren't even round anymore. I fell into the lure of commercials that told me that a sleeve of new balls would help my game – and I believed it. It didn't matter that I never took the time to go to the golf range. It didn't matter that my technique was so bad that I resembled a befuddled *base*-ketball player. It didn't matter that I didn't know the rules, nor did I care to. What mattered to me at that time was the projected flight pattern and backspin of these new Nike balls which should give me a softer landing onto the green.

I was beginning to hit the ball better. With my very limited skills I was actually sending the ball forward most of the time. Unlike most golfers who would arrive at the course roughly 30 to 45 minutes early to warm up and take practice swings, I would get to the course right before tee off, rush myself into the pro-shop to check in and hurry to the tee box. I would always declare two balls off the first tee box then proceed to hit the first one into the woods. The funny thing about that is after the bad hit I would frown and become angry; then look down at the club as if it had done something wrong.

Refusing to take a lesson and the reasoning behind it was really the product of two worlds colliding. Perfect practice makes perfect; and what I was attempting to do was just the complete opposite. The clouded confusion going on between my ears permitted me to accept my explanation of why I hit a good shot then question it heavily when I didn't. Did I want to improve my game? Sure I did, but I didn't want to spend a lot of time practicing to do it. I wanted the 'microwaveable' fun effect. I wanted to quickly improve to the point where I could be better than average...*YESTERDAY*! Why? Because I heard someone say that most golfers can't break 100 consistently and I wanted to be above average…all while having fun.

The more golf I played, the more people I met. The more people I met, the more I learned about golf's international appeal, which I enjoyed immensely. So to continue the joy I played more golf. The cold, stiff fence that once pressed against my face and felt my bony fingers piercing through its shell was now on my backside. I had penetrated the invisible wall of substance. No longer was I oblivious and/or dismissive of a world where your most elusive adversary is an incredibly large green mass with a bunch of sizeable muscles protruding from its skin and not named "Hulk".

The shift in my circle of friends became evident. I didn't consciously choose to be with one group more than the other but it was an unavoidable result. The more I was enjoying the game of golf the more I gravitated to those who shared my sentiments. I didn't even take offense when asked what my handicap was. The whirlwind I was caught up in felt good to my senses but it was creating an increasing rift with those who had commanded my time in the past. I quickly learned that everyone wasn't riding along on my meteoric shuttle ride to this new euphoria. Some even rejected a free ride. A line in the sand was being drawn and I tried repeatedly to erase it but I knew eventually the soft sand would turn to hard stone. I was hoping for the best and preparing for the worst; but none of that diminished my need to play.

My job allowed some flexibility in my schedule and wherever possible I was on the tee box. Technology was the reason I could operate autonomously and I believed in taking full advantage of all opportunities. My iPhone was a gift and a curse. Compliments of Steve Jobs, it provided me with the ability to access email and stay connected to the outside world but it also interrupted my concentration whenever there was an incoming inquiry. How dare they call me during my approach shot!

There were days when I would play 9 holes then have to rush out unexpectedly to change my clothes and see a client because of an escalated issue – only to arrive and discover that the issue was something that could have been handled via the phone, but it seems like a personal visit always calms an enraged client. I guess yelling at someone through a receiver does nothing for the inner psyche, even if the issue gets resolved, but a face-to-face "bitch session" works wonders. There were also days when the phone would lose its voice and I would be able to play all day. A normal round of golf is 18 incredible holes but when you are bordering the line of addiction you do what you have to do to be able to continue. I've had many days where I played 27 holes in the morning and then returned for another 18 in the late afternoon. I would never schedule such a day of determination with the course…it would just occur.

With each swing of the golf club my level of enjoyment continued to swell. Most of the constructive criticism I received about my game was put to very good use. I learned to use my 8 iron, instead of my pitching wedge around the green and it knocked at least 4 strokes off my scorecard. The straightening of my left arm and employing a stiffer shaft for my driver increased my yardage dramatically. As simple as it sounds, "Keep your head down" is one point I am trying to master; but I want to see where those new Nike balls are heading so I can retrieve them if need be.

Golf is such a mental game. It takes consistent focus and the ability to concentrate on every shot on every hole. Back to back miss-hits can screw up your scorecard, but even worse than that, playing on an open public course can screw up your life. The groups of guys that I played with that Saturday morning were also new amateurs who liked the game and decided to take it up to fill the void left from their professional football and UFC fighting careers.

Usually public courses are filled with all types of weekend warriors who drown their scorecard sorrows in the alcohol which is made readily available by the pretty young genie whose cart tends to appear just as the last swig of the previous beverage is consumed.

After we all managed to hit the fairway on hole 18 we sighed because our round was coming to a close. The maniacal group that had played behind us all day was becoming more and more impatient. While perched over his ball in the fairway about to make an approach shot to the green my UFC golf-cart partner raised his club above his right shoulder then started the clubs descent. Suddenly, out of nowhere, he was struck on the top of his head by a white flying object with dimples. Involuntarily, he took a quick power nap. When he arose from his short slumber he decided to pay a visit to the occupants of the tee box behind us.

Chapter 8

The Intervention

Work was becoming optional, even though my finances were in a headlock. I began to neglect my responsibilities, or at least put them on a "do-tomorrow" list. I quickly ramped up to playing twice a week and buying all sorts of assorted clubs on eBay. Before I knew it I had another set of clubs that were alien to one another. The impulsive actions I was displaying were reminiscent to those of a confused "crack head" yearning for relief from benzoylmethylecgonine.

My wife thought it was time for some intervention. After finding receipts for golf purchases hidden in my dress shoes, she decided that we needed some time away from our stressful environment. She assumed that removing me from the fray would allow me to have an "out of body" view of myself and my actions. I applaud her for thinking about me but I was upset at *what* she was thinking about me.

"Honey, I think it's time you and I take some time for ourselves and get away for a few days. Between work, kids and bills our stress levels have gone through the roof and it's necessary to take a time out," she said.

"I really don't need to go away. I just need a couple of days to collect my thoughts, gather myself and regroup. I can do that inexpensively by staying home and just playing a few rounds of golf. Maybe you can get some clubs and come play with me," I replied.

At that very moment the intervention took a turn for the worse. Even an underwater addict knows when he has pushed the envelope too far. From behind a face that looked like it had been smelling onions came these delightful words of encouragement, "Did you just ask me to spend a vacation playing golf? You must be out of your mind. I wasn't going to let the cat out of the bag about finding hidden golf receipts all over the place but the cat has is no longer meowing; it's BARKING! This golf stuff you are into was cool in the beginning but you are taking it to the extreme. It's way out of hand. You are like an addict and that little white ball is like your powder. I took the liberty of adding up the receipts I found and just in case you were not aware of it you are averaging two hundred bucks a week playing golf. That's ridiculous! Who does that? You're playing on big boy courses with a little leaguer's salary and to top it off you can't even keep your ball out of the bushes. This needs to S-T-O-P!"

I really believed I heard every word she pounded me with. It seemed like I was stuck in a foggy Twilight Zone. The Fourth Dimension I was rotating in and out of had me in a trance and all I could do was stand and nod. Little did she know that when you are in the Fourth Dimension your senses are a bit discombobulated.

What I really heard was, "Honey, I would love to play with you but you would probably have more fun with the guys. It would be a waste of time and money if I bought clubs. You should use that money to play on nicer courses. I see that you are really into playing and it would be selfish of me to try and keep you from having fun. The two hundred dollars you're spending to play is a ridiculously small sum for what you are getting in return. You are always thinking of others first and this need to S-T-O-P!"

What a wonderful woman. I am so lucky to have found someone who truly understands me. My nod went from a quick up and down motion to a slow side to side sway. Like a glitch in the Matrix I return to the present to find her sucking her teeth, rolling her eyes and storming out of the room. For the life of me I couldn't understand what made her become so emotional all of a sudden. We went from a nice pleasant conversation to her storming out saying, "What do you mean NO! How dare you tell me NO! I'm trying to help your crazy ass and you're standing there shaking your head, NO! I hope you break a club!"

WOMEN!!

I concluded that she stormed all the way to the mall to relieve her stress. It was bad, but it wasn't anything that R.H. Macy or William T. Dillard couldn't smooth over. I was still standing in the same position with my back up against the entry to the garage. I tried to propel myself forward by pressing both hands against the door and flexing my abdominal muscles for leverage but instead the door flew open and I fell backwards. I crash landed on my golf bag and was very thankful I had left it lying on the ground right in front of the steps. Or had I? I know I am not crazy but a faint voice whispered, "You're welcome!" Surprised, I quickly jumped to my feet and tried to remember my last encounter with my clubs. I ALWAYS place them in the right hand corner of the garage once I am done playing. Today they were in the middle of the floor near the door. Was my mind playing tricks on me? Did my clubs know I was going to fall through the door and did they lie down in between me and the ground to break my fall? Either way I was grateful; and to show them my appreciation I took them out for a scenic walk of approximately 6900 yards.

Chapter 9

Misery Loves Company

What began as an, "Oh what the hell, I'll try it once", has now morphed into an uncompromising obsession with no signs of tapering off. All I could think of was the next time I was going to be able to play. Since my game was getting a little better and I was just barely breaking 100 consistently on my scorecard, I felt I had earned the right to bring it up as topic of conversation. One day while at a neighborhood gym I ran into two friends who I had not seen in awhile.

"Hey wassup Miguel? Wassup Claude?"

I had met Miguel and Claude on the basketball court a few years ago when I moved away from the more urban parts of the Bay area. Both were weekend warriors such as me and their ages are just a few years north of mine. Both were born and raised in The South and were as comical as two guys can get without even knowing it. Miguel is a 6'2" reed-thin man with hints of gray around his hairline.

"Hey dude. Where have you been? Seems I haven't seen you in ages," he said.

"I know, it's been a long time. I have been just keeping busy. I started changing my routine up a bit. I haven't been playing too much basketball lately. I bought some golf clubs and I can't put them down. I played in a charity event about a year ago and I think I caught the fever!" I replied.

"GOLF?? YOU?? I would have never matched *those* two entities together" said Claude, who is an ex-military man. Standing about 5'9" with the R-O-T-C high and tight haircut and a personality the size of Texas, he listened as I responded, "I know! It's all like a whirlwind romance. I play whenever it's possible and I am working on some things to get better. It seems I have developed a left to right slice that is causing me a bit of grief."

"Are you keeping your head down, elbow straight and not opening up the club too soon?" he asked.

I looked at him with a perplexed stare, then responded, "You play?"

In unison they both confirmed, "Yes! Every weekend!"

My eyes widened in amazement. Golfers are hidden everywhere. They comprise many different types of people across multiple age groups and nationalities. I was ecstatic to find two good guys who were compatible with my personality and sense of humor and lived a short distance from me. The only remaining question was how I was going to break into their group of weekly players.

"What are you doing next weekend?" asked Miguel.

Like an excited child who has just been released from a parental punishment I immediately responded, "I'm free!" Miguel proceeded to invite me to join their weekly quest to play every course in Central Florida. I found that goal to be one of extreme excitement. Little did he know that I was all in even before he asked me. We exchanged phone numbers and they gave me the name and the address of the course where we would be playing.

"What is the tee time?" I asked.

"Tee time? We don't set tee times!"said Claude. "We just show up with our gear and then the people at the pro shop believe they missed something. They go out of their way to get us out as quickly as possible. Most of the time they even discount the rate to offset their 'error'. Genius, isn't it?"

RED FLAG NUMBER ONE!

The rising of the sun over the misty horizon signaled the arrival of a gorgeous Saturday morning. The smell of breakfast was dancing through the air as my wife had the overwhelming urge to delight us with her culinary skills instead of lying comatose and resting from a hard week of work. These are the times when life is great. I am able to wake up without any pain on a gorgeous day to a scrumptious meal cooked with love and then play golf with some good friends. What could be more enjoyable than this?

At approximately 9 o'clock I headed for the garage to pack my clubs and shoes into the rear of my car. I grabbed the cooler also, as it would be a great idea to ice down some water and Gatorade so that when we finish our round we would have something cold to drink. I kissed my wife goodbye and proceeded out the door and into the car heading towards the entry to Interstate 75 South.

A half hour later I exited the ramp, made a left at the traffic light, another left past the cart crossing sign, then a right into the Golf Club that I nicknamed "Terrorville" because of its consistent damage to my scorecard. I was quite hesitant to drive up to the baggage drop area and valet my car as the Starter was there checking in each four-man group. I decided to park in the general population area and walk my bag up the incline towards the pro-shop. As I arrived at the top of the hill I saw Miguel and Claude standing with the Starter.

"C'mon man. We're next on the tee box," shouted Miguel. Without a hitch in my step I hurried to their side as two attendants scurried to find additional golf carts for us to use. After loading our bags onto the back of the carts I noticed that Miguel and Claude also had ball retrievers and garbage bags in the basket area behind their seats. I dismissed it for now and began walking towards the Pro Shop to pay for my round.

"Where are you going? Everything is taken care of already!" said Claude.

"OK. Just tell me how much I owe you and we can settle up during the turn," I said.

Claude and Miguel just chuckled, "We have to teach the young fella a few things don't we, Claude?"

"Yeah. It sure seems that he's still moist behind the ears, Miguel."

RED FLAG NUMBER TWO!

The three of us head for the first tee box. Miguel and Claude are riding together and I'm riding alone. The order of play was set up by a genuine gesture from my heart, "Seniors before juniors, gentlemen."

Agreed!

Miguel was first to tee off. He swung his club and despite an ailing shoulder put his first tee shot at the 150 yard marker. Both Claude and I complimented his phenomenal achievement. Next, Claude got into position, swung his club and put his ball down the middle of the fairway right beside Miguel's! Again, we complimented a great shot. I approached the tee box with a bit of shaky confidence. I swung my driver and my first shot of the day landed left of the 150 yard marker but still in the fairway.

"Oh-oh Claude, seems we snagged a player, huh?" said Miguel.

It felt good to have that kind of start and to receive that kind of compliment. I put my driver back in my bag and plopped into the driver's seat of the cart and raced towards my ball. Following the designated cart path, we drove by a heavily wooded and marshy area. I noticed that Miguel and Claude were looking around as if their heads were on two swivels. It seemed a little odd to me at the time, but as I have gotten a bit older I have noticed that I too have my odd and quirky moments. We came up onto our balls, which were all lying nicely within the fairway with a great open shot at the green. I pressed down hard on the brake pedal to stop my cart and when I turned my head to the right to make a comment to the fellas I became frozen with what I saw.

Before their cart came to a complete stop Miguel and Claude had jumped out, grabbed their respective ball retrievers and garbage bags and headed in different directions – Miguel to the woods and Claude to the lake.

"What the hell are ya'll doing?" I shouted in confusion.

"We gotta get our hunt on!" yelled Miguel, "Last week we found a total of 155 balls. No need to purchase brand new ball when there are dozens of one-hitter-quitters out here!"

"You guys are kidding me, right?" I received no answer.

Miguel had disappeared into the brush and Claude was extending his ball retriever to the limit with both feet submerged in the water.

"Reach in the back of our cart and get that other bag for yourself. It's a gold mine out here," he shouted.

I stood in a state of shock and disbelief. Here I am standing in the middle of the fairway with two carts and no other players. I looked behind me and could see the next group behind us warming up on the tee box.

"Hurry up guys, there is another group waiting to tee off!" I screamed. I was feeling like the lookout guy during a bank heist. A few moments later both guys raced back towards their cart carrying ten to twelve golf balls each.

"OK! Now that is a honey hole," said Miguel as he retrieved his club to hit his second shot.

"I agree," said Claude as he followed Miguel's lead. With both men hitting their second shots onto the green it was my turn to follow the leaders. I set up over my ball and tried to block out what I had just seen. It was extremely difficult to erase the vision of two men jumping out of a moving cart and frolicking in the non-golf areas as if they worked on the course. Now add to that the fact that the group behind us was watching our every move as we held up play... and you can guess the outcome of my rushed and unfocused second shot – a slice which rolled across the right side of the fairway and into the pond.

DAMN!

"I'll get it. Toss another ball down and hit again!" said Claude. He pulled out his trusty retriever again and headed for the water as if he were *Aqua Man*. No sooner had I hit my second shot onto the green than Claude was throwing my first ball back at me.

"Nice shot bro! Here is your first ball!" I hopped into my cart, dumbfounded and a bit annoyed. I was hoping that this was a 'first hole occurrence' only and that the dynamic duo would not be prancing into the outer realms of Gotham to tackle the off-fairway villains and rescue every small, round, white-dimpled munchkin they could find.

I was wrong.

With each passing hole it seemed they would go further and further into the abyss. Their once- empty Glad bags were filling up very quickly and they were excited about the possibility of wiping the course clean. Miguel and Claude had their 'process' down to a science. Never before had I seen such collaboration and results-oriented focus on the golf course. I began to sit back in my cart and marvel at what was taking place after each swing of the club. I couldn't help but wonder if they really paid to play golf and hopefully find balls or was it that they paid to find balls and if time permitted then they played golf?

The answer to my question actually materialized while we were playing hole number 16. During one of their off-course excursions, Claude found an area that had corralled a huge number of lost golf balls. In a wooded patch just off the right side of the fairway, where every right-left slice would land, lay approximately forty bleached white one-hitters. Similar to predators feeding on a large carcass, the awesome twosome set up camp and began dining on their prey. They were so gluttonous that they totally ignored the repeated cry that someone was on the tee box awaiting clearance to tee off. Instead I heard a voice coming from the darkness instructing me to wave my hand and signal the group to play through us.

Fifteen minutes later my two golf buddies emerged from the wilderness with thorns piercing their clothes and enormous smiles on their faces. You would think by their behavior that they'd just hit a lottery jackpot or robbed a bank. They were so satisfied with their findings that they even questioned finishing the remaining two holes.

"You guys are unbelievable!" I said.

"You better hop on the train, dude. We just got paid for playing golf," said Miguel. "When you play for free then make a killing like we did, you come out ahead. Yep, they sure paid me to play today!"

On the drive home all I could do was laugh. Sure, I played bad today and failed to break 100 on my scorecard but who in their right mind can stay focused when there are people disappearing and reappearing all over the course? I tossed my scorecard into the trash, but what I experienced that day will last forever.

Chapter 10

A New Day

The more things change, the more they stay the same. Golf had filled the void that once was occupied by basketball. Growing up in an area where stress-filled days gave way to restless nights, the parallelogram which used to be my safe haven had become just four elongated lines that constantly chased each other. As I see it, my fateful date with golf was part of the natural growth progression of my character.

When I run the perceptions of each sport through a parallel comparison it's at that moment when the lights flash and the path is clear. It's at that moment when the fog is most transparent and its meaning is most comprehensive. In the eyes of society, for the most part golf is considered to be the more sophisticated of the two. Golf can be played by people of any age regardless of their athletic ability. They generally conduct themselves in a quieter, more subdued manor. It symbolizes the realm of personal growth.

Basketball, on the other hand, is viewed by most to be the embodiment of the youthful spirit of hip hop and social media. Defiant and highly interactive during my earlier years leading up to adulthood, I sought refuge with what I coveted through my window. Roundball echoed my sentiments loudly and together we forged a path through difficult times, awkward experiences, disappointments and triumphs.

Now as I age I acknowledge that a transition is taking place within my life that is giving birth to an entirely new individual. My likes and dislikes, worldly views, tolerance levels and emotional capacities are all in a state of change. It is more than just the process of maturation. It's a next level transformation! And what I am excited about is that I am at ease with it all.

So you ask, do I love basketball? *Yes!* Do I still love to play? *Yes!* Will I ever completely stop playing? *Probably not!* Together we have too much history. Although golf is slowly becoming my new basketball, I truly believe there is room for both in my life. I prefer to use one for stress relief and keep the other one in my back pocket for those days when I'm craving raw competition. Since my body is past the age of a gray-less chin and rock hard abdominal muscles I find that I hover more on the side of stress relief.

My personality has always been one of overindulgence. Once I find something that I like, or something that makes me feel good inside, I try to do it often so as to keep the feeling consistent. One can say that I've overdosed on golf in the short amount of time since its introduction into my life. Usually the cycle starts with a *"feeler"* to see if I enjoy what I'm doing. Next comes the *"routine"* of implementing it into my everyday life. From here it either levels out to be something I can handle and will do on occasion or it rockets itself into a frenzy with an addictive type of effect. It's at this stage where I become fanatical and begin trying to squeeze every ounce of enjoyment out of it until the proverbial "*burnout*" occurs.

I felt a burning desire to explain this to my buddies, as I wanted to clear the air of any misconceptions about my recent absences, non- returned phone calls and emails. I decided to call my buddy, Steve, and thank him for the unique window of opportunity he gave to me and the necessary push to jump through it. Little did I know about the magnitude one chance outing with the fellas would have on my existence. He certainly deserved another "*Thank you*" from me, as golf is one thing that I know I need to do more of. In complete anticipation of sharing my newfound joy I picked up the receiver and began dialing his number. In my mind I pictured Steve sitting in his office trying to uncover another opportunity to propel life forward. His muscle head, swaying back and forth, would be applying enormous pressure to the seams of his fitted cap. The pulsating key chimes suddenly progressed to a ringing and the connection was confirmed. I positioned the words of thanks into my voice box and was all but ready to release them when I heard, "Yabba Dabba Doo Dawg! It's you know who! Forget what you heard and recall what you already knew! It's unfortunate for you to have reached my voicemail and I know that you're upset, 'cause you're expecting to speak to Fred and he hasn't answered yet. But

hold the phone tight and please do not weep because you
can begin to leave a message in 3-2-1 beeeeeeeeeeeeeep!"